The Seed
of
Imagination

AGGIE UNDA

Love inspires.

To my children, for being your unique wonderful selves:

I loved you even before I knew you

I love you to the moon and back

I am a better person, a better mother,
a better human being because of you.

To Alberto, the love of my life:

Thank you for your constant support
and for always believing in me

I love you more.

From the Author

This is a work of fiction inspired by my two children. My son is in the autism spectrum, and many of the experiences lived throughout this adventure are based on my life as an autism mom—what I see, think and feel go through his mind as we experience this wonderful world together. There is also the relationship full of love and patience that my beautiful daughter has with her brother, and how magical their imagination is.

Thank you for sharing with me the mysterious and wonderful world of autism, individuality and uniqueness.

Much love,
Aggie Unda

Before You Begin Reading

The adventure you're about to experience will definitely be understood and enjoyed even more with further knowledge of what autism is. This story is narrated by our main character, who is in the autism spectrum, and will at times take you on an adventure of what is happening inside of his mind.

There are discussion questions at the end of each chapter. These are meant to open up communication between the child and his or her teacher, parent or even with himself or herself. There are no right or wrong answers. If you wish, feel free to skip them altogether, go straight into the next chapter, and come back to them at the end of the book.

Hang on tight and set your mind free as you discover *The Seed of Imagination*.

What Is Autism?

Autism spectrum disorder (ASD) is a difference in the way a kid's brain develops. Kids with autism may have trouble understanding the world around them. Kids with autism might have trouble:

- Talking and learning the meaning of words.
- Making friends or fitting in.

- Dealing with changes (like trying new foods, having a substitute teacher, having their toys moved or a change in routine).
- Dealing with loud noises, bright lights or crowds.

Kids might also move in an unusual way (like flapping their hands or rocking), or do the same thing over and over (like saying the same word).

A kid with autism may have a little trouble with these things or a lot. Some kids may need only a little bit of help, and others might need a lot of help with learning and doing everyday stuff.

What Causes Autism?

Autism is something people are born with. No one knows exactly what causes it. It probably has something to do with a kid's genes and other things that change the way the brain develops.

How Is Autism Disorder Treated?

There is no cure for autism, but treatment can make a big difference. The younger kids are when they start treatment, the better.

Doctors, therapists and special education teachers can help kids learn to talk, play and learn. Therapists also help kids learn about making friends, taking turns and getting along.

What If My Friend Has Autism Spectrum Disorder?

All people deserve respect, but kids with ASD may be teased, bullied or left out because they're different. Bullying and teasing are never the right way to treat other people, but it may be hard to be a friend with someone who has ASD.

Kids with ASD often don't understand playful jokes. You may need to be very clear when you communicate with someone who has ASD.

Try to be patient and kind. Remember how hard it might be for the person with ASD to understand how to be a friend. Stand up for classmates who are bullied. Tell adults, so they can help protect kids who are bullied.

Reviewed by Diane E.Treadwell-Deering, MD, March 2019

kidshealth.org

This is not meant to diagnose and/or treat autism. It is simply a brief informative description of autism for the better understanding of this work of fiction

WHO STOLE THE SEED OF IMAGINATION? SOLVING THE RIDDLE

I closed my eyes and the rhythmic sound of my own humming was the only thing I could hear. Wanted to hear.... As I rocked my body back and forth and closed my eyes, everything seemed better, calmer, peaceful, and my body began to relax. I saw beautiful colors in my mind mixing with one another, colors I can never quite create with my own paint box.

The colors then turn into shapes, and the shapes, soon after, turn into patterns one after another. I had my very own 3D slideshow inside my head. I don't know how much time passed, since time is difficult for me to understand, when I suddenly felt my body tensing again as my sister removed my hands from my eyes, and stood in front of me with her hands on her waist waiting for an answer. I stared at her, not knowing at all what the question had been, but as I was staring back at her, I noticed how different the color of her eyes looked against the sunlight. Immediately, I turned to my desk and tried to mix the correct paint colors, in order to create the color of her eyes. I knew she was saying something while I was doing this, but it sounded all mumbled, and whatever it was, it could not be more important than this. She finally said my name, and that got my attention.

"Well?" she said again.

"Well, what?" I answered, not knowing what was she waiting for?

"Well, what do you think?" she snapped back, with an exasperated look on her face.

I had no idea what she was talking about, but I really needed to get her eye color done properly. It was a mix of raw honey with amber, and her right eye was a tad bigger than the left. That bothered me sometimes, but my mom said not to give it much importance, that everyone had one eye bigger than the other...what?! That, of course did not make me feel better at all—everybody, including me, was walking around with different sized eyes. Remembering that made my heart begin to beat faster again, so I immediately reached into my pocket to hold on to the rainbow fluorite stone I carry with me all the time, and as I felt the smooth texture, she repeated "Well?!"

"Well what?" I said again, clueless of what she was talking about.

"Mom said to water our flower and it's not on the windowsill. So, where is it?"

I turned my head towards the window, expecting to see the beautiful multi-colored flower mom gave us years ago. "Well, it should be there," I said.

"But it's not" responded Kaia.

I suddenly imagined two little legs growing from the flower pot, running around the room trying to hide. That, of course made me laugh out loud, which deeply annoyed my sister. "Why are you laughing?!" she snapped with confusion and annoyance in her eyes.

That made her eye color change again...hmmm, interesting. I got closer to her to get a better look at the new eye color when she started to pace around the room looking for the flower.

"Are you just going to stand there, or are you actually going to help me look?" she said. "You know how important that flower is to mom."

We looked everywhere! Well, actually, Kaia looked everywhere and I just stood in the middle of the room, turned 360 degrees and said "Nope, it's not here."

Kaia and I share a bedroom. It has two twin beds side by side. We actually measured and marked the middle of the room, so there would be no fighting or confusion. I knew mom would be upset when we drew the halfway division line with a permanent marker. After dividing our bedroom— perfectly evenly, may I add—I went downstairs and told her that we had split the bedroom in half. I was right, she was upset. I don't like it when my mom gets upset, it hurts my heart, but I can never seem to find the correct words to tell her how I feel. Sometimes I'm not even sure what I'm feeling either. Anyway, in front of the beds there is a bay window, and right there in the center we have... had...our flower. It was always bathed during the day with the warm sunlight, and at night, the moonlight shone at an angle, managing to brighten it up like a night light. Kaia has paintings of it everywhere. It was her favorite thing to paint and draw, until she got a bit older, thought she was too cool and started to paint other things. We of course have other things in our room: a dresser that measures the exact height of when I was seven, shelves where my thirteen teddy bears fit perfectly and in order of size, and our laundry basket—which never seems to have a fixed spot or be serving its purpose, and that bothers me.

Kaia did look. She crouched and bent, she jumped and searched, but was not able to find it. I was still standing in the middle of the room as she came closer to me. She is one of the few people that I don't mind getting close to—she always smells like a mix of caramel and strawberry, and knows not to be too loud when she's near me. Except when I make her angry, and she will then scream and that, my friends, make my ears hurt.

"Oooh mom is going to be mad if we don't find it," she said. "Do you remember when she gave it to us, years ago, when we were really young?"

Of course I remembered, not only because I'm older than Kaia, but because I have a really good memory.

"Can you tell me again the exact words she said?" asked my sister. I then began to repeat them, word by word. "Kids, this flower was born from a very special seed, the Seed of Imagination.

We all have it within us, it can take us to incredible places and we can create marvelous things with it."

"Yes!" said Kaia, "and it was always right here." She pointed to the window sill where there was no trace of our flower. I clearly remembered seeing how every time I watered it, it became brighter and bigger. I remember it well, since I had to go back to my colors and tune the mixture of the paint every time it changed— which to my annoyance, was constantly. Also, every time the flower was close to us, our imagination would take us to wonderful and magical places. At first, I thought it was only me, because I tend to "see" things differently, but one day, when Kaia was a lot younger, she told me that she knew that our flower was magical...that she could feel it.

"We have to find it!" I blurted out of blue and started looking, and moving things around trying to find it. As we kept looking, my sister (who is definitely the smartest person I know) searched under the bed.

"Wooooow..." I heard her say in slow motion. "Look what I found?"

Of course thinking it was our flower, I turned around only to find her holding...what was that?

As if reading my mind, she explained, "It's our ship's rudder. You see? Remember when we used to play that we were pirates and had that secret password that made the ship appear?"

As if taken from a dream, I remembered. "Yes!" That dream-like image became more real. I loved becoming a pirate, going to faraway lands, conquering obstacles and discovering treasure chests. Suddenly an unpleasant feeling in the pit of my stomach began to grow, and I could hear a tune, far away in the distance. Music I knew but couldn't place. I quickly shut my eyes and covered my ears and began to hum and rock back and forth.

Kaia rushed to me, and being careful not to touch me— since she knew better—soothed me and softly said my name. "Risho," she whispered.

But between my humming and the music, I couldn't hear her. The low-pitched music became louder as an unclear image popped into my head. I tried to substitute that image with my beautiful watercolor shapes and patterns, but he kept pushing them away.

"Risho!" she said with a stern voice.

My eyes flew open and my humming became louder.

"Sh...sh...sh...sh." Kaia repeated those words she had learned from watching mom.

"It's him! I exclaimed.

Kaia was focused on calming me down, and began breathing deeply as I copied her pattern—breathe in, breathe out. I calmed down and repeated, "It's him."

"Who are you talking about?" asked Kaia.

"Remember how the rudder got destroyed?" I asked.

"Yes, playing," she answered immediately.

I continued with a stutter, since my brain was thinking faster than I could speak. "The rain, the rain helped us."

"What are you talking about?" she said, starting to lose her patience.

Looking around and trying to find the correct words, I explained. "We fought against him in the storm..."

Like switching on a light bulb, she responded, "The evil magician! That's right! That's how the rudder got destroyed! We beat him!"

"Yes, we got him," I said, taking the rudder from my sister's hands. I slowly walked towards the window, searching deep within my brain. "He said something just as we defeated him." I couldn't quite find the memory I was looking for, when the same music began to play again in my head.

As I was reaching for my ears to cover them, my sister quietly asked, "Do you hear that?"

I turned to her. "You hear it too?"

"Yes," she whispered. "Where is that music coming from?"

As she said that, a warm breeze entered the room and filled it with these words:

> *Under the rain I will go because I have magic*
> *no more but the Seed of Imagination will*
> *travel with me to a different location.*

I turned and looked at the closed window and tried to figure out what was going on, when my sister exclaimed, "It's a riddle!" I was still overwhelmed and confused, but her mind was already making sense of what had happened.

"It's a riddle" she repeated.

I hated riddles. What was the point of them? If you wanted to say something, well, why not just say what it is, why have people guessing—and worst, why did people like guessing? While thinking about this and not understanding why people liked riddles, my sister brought me back to what was happening. "Remember that day? We beat the magician when the storm began..."

The images were clearer in my mind now. "Yes" I confirmed.

"It was because he ran out of magic!" she said. "He has no magic when it's raining. That's how we were able to defeat him that day."

"You're right," I said. "But still, where is the Seed of Imagination?" I sat on my bed and sighed.

I love my bed; it is probably my favorite place in the world. It is so soft and it has six blankets, which of course need to go in a particular order. I don't like it when mom has to change the sheets, because my favorites are the red ones, and on top of the sheet goes the thinnest white blanket (which it already has a hole, but I don't mind), and then a soft cream-colored one, which reminds me of the beach, but without the mess. Then, a knitted blue one (because blue is my favorite color), and on top of that my super-plush extra-big Star Wars blanket—because, I mean, who doesn't like Star Wars? And to top it off, a blue-weighted blanket with tiny silver stars. Ahhh, with these, I cover myself up completely and wrap myself up at night like a tight burrito. My mom always worries that I can't breathe covered up like that, and I know that every night, she comes in, turns off my star projector, finds a hole in my burrito blanket wrap and opens it wider for me to breathe. I don't get it—does she really think I would wrap myself purposely so I can't breathe? Deep in thought, and questioning myself with that, my sister calls, "Come quick, look what I found!"

I see her crawling like a worm under the dresser, and out she comes with a petal in her hand.

"That's a petal from our flower," I said. It's the most beautiful thing you have ever seen. It's deep blue with purple and pink mixed together like a watercolor wash, but, when the moonlight hits the petals you can see small specks that glitter as if they were tiny stars that lived there and the flower was its universe.

"It's so beautiful," my sister said. She carefully put the petal away in a small purse, where she carries her important things. "He took it...the evil magician took our flower."

Chapter 1
Discussion Questions

1. Do you have, or have you had, anything that you carry around to comfort yourself?

2. Some autistic people rock back and forth and hum. This is self-soothing, like taking a deep breath or counting to ten. What do you do to calm yourself down?

3. Usually the senses from kids in the spectrum are very sensitive. Our main character can pick up on the slightest smell. His sister smells to him like strawberry and caramel. Can you describe the smell of some of your favorite people? Try to match a smell to them.

4. Why do you think our main character shuts his eyes and covers his ear when he feels overwhelmed?

5. People in the spectrum are very literal and have a difficult time understanding jokes. That is why riddles bother him. Do you like riddles?

THE ADVENTURE BEGINS:
WHERE TO?

I knew what we had to do, and it had to be done. I turned to my sister, and she was already looking at me, waiting for me to say it. "Do you want to go on a pirate adventure?" I asked.

Her smile lit up her face, which again made her eye color change (so I took a mental note of that). "Let's do it!" Kaia said excitedly.

We both instinctively knew what we had to do. Each of us jumped on our beds facing the window. Kaia turned to me and said, "Ready captain!" And then, in unison, with our eyes closed and our hands reaching towards the sky and without even thinking twice, we exclaimed:

"One two three, pirate ship come to me! Four five six, get on board and do the twist! Seven eight nine, take us to a different time! Aaaaand ten ten ten!!!!"

I started to feel that tingly sensation in my hands and we both opened our eyes. The mysterious deep sound of a faraway boat horn was heard, as silk-like colors began to fill the room—

first, a deep rich royal purple rose from the ground up, brushing our eyesight, followed by a curtain of midnight blue that filled the whole room. Everything was still as the creaking sound of old wood cracked under the sound of crashing waves. Intense fog crept from under the door into our room, bringing in the salty smell of the sea. The temperature dropped slightly and the voices of a dozen men were heard in the background as they cried "Pull! Pull! Pull!" in deep voices. The sounds that made the hairs on my arm prickle were the deep trumpets that began to play in perfect harmony with the men like chorus orders of pulling.

Pirate ship sails began to drop, multi-colored fabric dancing and turning in the breeze as a mast rose from the ground and the sails took their place instinctively. Ropes that smelled of clams and salt tied the sails tightly in order to be able to support the strong ocean winds. As the ship began to take shape, the walls in our room dissolved under the salty waters, and a beautiful mermaid—with a shimmery turquoise golden tail decorated the bow, her tranquil eyes and soft smile made me feel at ease—as the music began to change again. The metal trumpets faded in the wind, and the breeze brought the chords of a violin to life with a soothing sound. No more voices were heard, no more soft blankets to stand on, just the hard wooden rudder that appeared right in front of me waiting to gain control of the ship as my sister and I sailed into the starry night.

The soft wind played with Kaia's curls, making them dance all around her face, while the breeze whispered lullabies into my ears. Dolphins, happy to see us, flanked our ship, leaving a long, sparkling wake behind them. The minutes ticked by, one at a time until they became hours, and by then, the only thing that accompanied us like a loyal soldier was the wind. Doubt crept on us like a crab creeps on a rock, smoothly, silently and unexpectedly.

"Where are we heading to?" asked Kaia, trying to make her voice as controlled as possible.

"I don't know," was my honest answer.

"Where shall we look?" Kaia continued with the interrogation.

"I don't know," I said again.

"Well, where's the magician?" she insisted.

"I don't know! I don't know! I don't know!" I exclaimed, letting go of the rudder and covering my ears.

Kaia didn't say another word. She kept her gaze locked on the horizon, and her breathing as calm as she possibly could considering that we were in the middle of the ocean not knowing where to look or go.

Time went by and nothing. Stillness was the only thing that surrounded us. Personally, I liked it; it was peaceful and calming. But as soon as I was relaxing into this feeling, Kaia pointed at something and yelled, "Watch out!"

As fast as I could, I turned the rudder. She pulled ropes and changed the sails, making the ship turn so that we wouldn't crash onto the dock that appeared out of thin air. The mermaid in the bow, with her calm eyes, slowly started facing a different direction in the compass.

Chapter 2
Discussion Questions

1. How do you think Kaia felt, not knowing where to look and or go, and not being able to talk about it with her brother?

2. Why do you think our main character likes it when it's quiet? Do you prefer a quiet atmosphere, or do you like having music, the TV or noise in the background?

THE JUGGLER:
FOLLOWING YOUR DREAMS

The ship was now gently standing right next to the dock, but we were still panting and trying to catch our breath. Even though it was dark, and I can't see as well as a cat at night, I did spot someone walking along the dock.

"Who's he?" I asked my sister.

"And what's he doing?" she questioned me back.

A tall, thin young man was walking along the dock looking up, not even watching where he was going. He had light brown hair and golden skin, his loose pants were rolled up almost to his knees and his feet were covered with sand—he probably had been walking on the beach. The sleeves of his white shirt were also rolled up and one of his hands was placed above his eyes, clearly looking for something in the sky.

Kaia and I simultaneously looked up following his gaze, but didn't see anything unusual in the night sky. We got off the ship and walked to the edge of the dock, where he was still looking up. We got closer to him, but he didn't seem to notice.

"Hi," my sister said softly.

He hadn't even realized that he was not standing alone anymore. I got right behind him, tapped him on the shoulder, and loudly said "Hello!"

He was so startled that he jumped, yelled and turned, all at the same time. It was so funny that we started laughing. "Oh hi! I didn't see you there" he said.

"What's your name?" I asked.

"Alex," he said, stretching his hand out for me to shake. Remembering and quickly going over the hand-shaking rules in my head, I grasped his hand in a tight but not too tight grip, looked him directly in the eye—which is very uncomfortable to me, but everyone keeps explaining how important it is and to do it, so I try my best. I count two seconds for the shake—up, down, one, two, stare and then I release with a frozen, unnatural smile. Kaia does the same, but much more comfortably and with a genuine smile.

"What are you doing?" she asked Alex

"I'm looking for my juggling clubs, but I can't find them." He returned his gaze upwards.

Again, not making sense of what he was saying, my sister continued, "Clubs? What for?"

As soon as Alex heard that, he very slowly lowered his gaze, turned to Kaia and walked straight to her.

"What do you mean what for?" he asked in disbelief and in utter confusion.

"Well, yes," continued Kaia, "if you can't find them, why don't you just do something else?"

"No no no, you don't understand—when I'm juggling, I'm happy!"

Alex tried to explain, but Kaia continued "why don't you try other things?"

Alex almost cut her off mid-sentence with his answer. "But I have!" he said. "I've tried everything, but it's not the same! This makes me feel happy, really really happy. Clubs, rings, balls it doesn't matter, when I'm juggling I feel as if time stands still and flies, all at the same time! Everything outside of me is a blur and I'm happy being me just where I'm at. I even catch myself smiling. Have you ever felt that?"

Kaia shook her head slightly, almost unnoticeably.

His question got me thinking, and I quickly concluded that I like it when people smile, but my sister, for the first time, didn't say anything back. "We'll help you find them!" I said confidently.

"Yes, of course," my sister joined in, but not as bubbly as she usually would. "When was the last time you saw them?"

Alex thought for a second, and without saying a word started to walk away, and away and away. When we realized he was not coming back, it took some quick running to catch up with him. "What are you doing?" asked Kaia, not feeling amused at all.

"You specifically asked me where was the last time that I had seen them, and it was certainly not over there where I was standing, so I'm going to where I last had them with me."

Well, that did make sense.

"Now," Alex continued, "I was standing right here juggling rings, clubs and balls, learning and trying out new tricks." I could see the excitement in his eyes when he went through his movements. "I started to throw the clubs higher and higher in the air, swiftly changing hands and passing them so fast. It was the highest I had ever thrown them!" he said, smiling. "I couldn't believe it, it was as if they were touching the sky!"

Kaia and I felt Alex's excitement, but as he continued, his eyes saddened. "Suddenly, they never fell back down, so I repeated the same motions with the rings and the balls, higher and higher each time. Again, they stayed up there, in the sky."

"What do you mean?" I asked, not fully understanding.

"I know how gravity works, and the clubs, rings and balls should have just fallen back down," Kaia said in her know-it-all tone. "Now, depending on speed, weight and height, according to my calculations, the..."

She got cut off by Alex. "They just stayed up there and didn't fall back down," he said.

The three of us at the same time and very slowly lifted our gaze to the sky. It was beautiful. Millions of stars decorated the night. As we looked at this painted canvas, our jaws dropped in amazement. "Wow" was the only thing we could articulate, without peeling our eyes from the night sky.

"And now," Alex sighed, "I just don't know what to do." He turned to look at us asking for help with his eyes.

"Don't worry," I jumped in, trying to make him feel better, and I gave him a smile.

But Kaia kept staring at the sky. Honestly, I found it odd that Kaia kept staring into space like that, but hey, who am I to judge? We all have our quirks and she, well, she likes staring into space, deep in thought may I add.

So I continued. "We'll find them," I said.

"You'll help me?" asked Alex hopefully.

"Of course we will!" I said.

We turned to Kaia and found her still staring up. I saw Alex pull in air to his lungs to speak, when suddenly, "Look!" Kaia exclaimed, pointing to the sky.

Alex and I both looked up.

"The stars have them," she continued, with a smile on her face. Have you noticed how eyes twinkle when people are smiling? It almost seems to reflect the twinkle from the stars. That's what Kaia held in her eyes at that moment.

"I don't see anything." Alex interrupted my thoughts.

I looked up and didn't see anything either.

"The fact that you don't see it, doesn't mean it isn't there," Kaia said, pointing to the stars. "Right there! Do you see it?"

Alex and I shook our heads.

We then heard a swishing sound, followed by Kaia's giggle. "Look again," she said. "Look where you haven't seen before."

We looked up again, and heard soft, musical piano notes playing and a swishing sound that left a trail that the three of us were able to follow with our eyes.

"Did you see that?" I said in awe. "Did you see that!?" I repeated.

Kaia and Alex both nodded, and again the swishing sound was heard. It sounded like a ball being thrown by a pitcher going as fast as 100 miles an hour. It was like being in a baseball field with professional super-strength pitchers. In unison, the three of us followed the swooshing sound from one side to another, our heads turning with it.

"The stars are playing with them!" I couldn't help but laugh as I witnessed this

But Alex was not smiling, and was not amused at all. "The stars took them!" he remarked. "Just you wait until I get my hands on one of you!" he said angrily to the stars, jumping up and down, trying to grab one of them. "And when I do, I will break those pointy little arms of yours and you will glow no more!"

I could see Kaia's eyes grow big and I immediately knew what was coming. "No!" she snapped back. "You can't hurt them, they are too important and beautiful, and they shine their own light."

"Yes," I continued. "They were our guide during the night, and led us here. To you." I closed my eyes and sighed. "Besides, I make a wish every night to the first star I see."

I could see Alex's eyes begin to water. I thought he had been staring too hard at the stars and it had irritated his eyes. If that were the case, he really should have them checked out by a professional. But Kaia asked, "Alex, why are you crying?"

"They took from me my most loved possession," he answered as a tear rolled down.

"You're right," said Kaia with that wisdom in her eyes that is sometimes really not age appropriate. "That was wrong, very wrong. But we'll talk to them and get it all sorted out." We all looked up as she softly said, "Hi, twinkling stars."

There was a pause—a very long pause. We looked at each other and Kaia smiled nervously.

"Stars," she said louder and firmer. Nothing. "Staaars!" she exclaimed loudly.

Alex and I looked at each other, hiding our smiles from her, and turned to look up again.

Amazingly, the swishing stopped, and the stars focused their attention on her. "Stars," Kaia continued in her friendly voice, "our friend misses his juggling clubs, rings and balls, and loves what he does very much. It makes him happy and fulfilled. It is very important that you give them back."

Suddenly we saw something falling from the sky, getting closer and closer just like a shooting star. Alex knew what it was, and put his hand out to catch them. One, two, three, four, five clubs fell from the sky, and Alex caught them all with incredible speed and coordination. Then came the rings, and finally the balls.

Kaia thanked the stars and reminded them not to take things without permission. They all agreed with happy jingles. We said goodbye to the stars, and we could see how happy Alex was.

"Thank you," he said to us with a huge smile.

"You're welcome, that's what friends are for. We help one another," said Kaia in return. Excitement filled Alex's eyes. He told us to take a seat and that he would be right back.

I looked around in order to sit down, but the only thing I saw was sand, sand everywhere and I was not properly dressed to have sand all over me. Kaia sat and started playing with the sand, waiting for Alex. He had said he would be back sooner than I would think. Well, I thought, and Alex was not back. Sitting down was the only option, but there were no chairs or towels to sit on. I was going to get sand all over me, and that made me uncomfortable. I reached into my pocket to touch the fluorite stone, which immediately soothed me. Fortunately, I saw Alex walking back with a towel, and more of his juggling equipment. I spread the towel on even surface and sat down trying to keep all the sand clear from it.

Alex was radiating excitement, and as a thank you for our help he wanted to perform for us. I liked the idea very much. It was able to pull me from the darkness that started to creep inside me and enjoy a little bit of magic.

When he caught the last club in his hand, Alex was gleaming, and I could feel golden sparks coming out of him. Kaia was clapping with a huge grin on her face. "That was spectacular!" Kaia told him. We explained to him that we had to continue our travels, and set sail. "We have lost something and need to find it," Kaia explained.

"What is it?" Alex asked, intrigued.

She told him everything about the Seed of Imagination, but as she was telling the story the only thing I kept thinking was, we didn't lose it, it was stolen! I interrupted the story to say, "The magician stole it." I felt a huge weight in my heart when I realized I had no idea what I was doing, or where to look for it. My heart ached, and I think it's what they call sadness. I again reached into my pocket to get the fluorite stone, took it out and held it tight in my hand, but nothing happened, it was not working. Oh no, here it came...my sight began to blur, the sound of the ocean waves got louder and louder, and it felt as if they were crashing inside my thoughts. The sparks from the bonfire we had hissed at me, and the reds, yellows and oranges from it became brighter, too bright for me that my eyes began to hurt. I covered my ears and shut my eyes to block out the exterior world but I could still hear Alex's voice ringing in my ears asking what was wrong with me. I sat down right there in the middle of the beach, sand everywhere, and each grain of sand felt as if sandpaper was rubbing against my skin. My exposed arms felt raw from the touch of the sand, and I thought blood would soon start trickling. Oh no please let there be no blood. I can't handle blood. My humming became louder and my rocking became faster. Think, color patterns, color patterns, hum, rock, patterns, rock, colors, patterns, hum. I knew I was losing it. I started to feel how my cells began to detach from my body, floating out into the universe, my heart beat quickening. Something stung my eyes and was burning down my cheeks. Tears. I couldn't cover my ears and my eyes at the same time, so I kept switching back and forth, eyes, ears, loud, hot, I was getting ready to scream when suddenly I felt a warm golden cocoon bring me back together in a tight grip, keeping me from evaporating into the atmosphere. Sh... sh...sh...sh...sh...sh with a soft rocking and tight grip around me, slowly—very, very slowly—I felt how pieces of me began to go back to their place. Breathe in, breathe out, in and out, Kaia repeated. I was back. I was safe.

When Kaia saw me take out the stone, she knew I was trying to soothe myself, but when the rocking and the loud humming began, she stopped completely, not even listening to Alex's confusion about what was happening. But when I started to cry, she knew she had to act quickly, before it escalated even further.

She grabbed her towel and shook it briskly, making sure there was not a grain of sand stuck to it, and then wrapped the towel tightly around me and sat behind me hugging me tight, as tight as she could. Even though she's smaller than me, she made herself so big, like a bear, and she gave me a big, tight, warm bearhug. And with a soft, controlled voice she whispered in my ear what I had to do. Breathe.

Alex was standing there, not knowing what had just happened. "He's autistic," she said.

Alex's stare was still completely blank.

"His brain just has a different method of working," she said, "and sometimes his senses get an overload of information. My brother can sometimes handle this, and has his own coping methods, but at times it might just be too much and has a meltdown. That's what just happened, and I helped him pull himself back together. It's not something he voluntarily chooses to do."

"Is he OK?" asked Alex,

"Of course he's OK!" said my sister. She sometimes gets annoyed when people look at me differently. "He's just like you and me. He's a regular boy! He just thinks and reacts differently in situations, and that makes him so unique and awesome. The world sometimes can't handle different, but that's their loss."

I hadn't heard a word she said. The only thing I kept thinking was that we needed to find the magician and recover our flower. "Let's go, Kaia" I said.

Suddenly, as if struck by lightning, Alex said, "hold on! You said 'magician,' right?"

We both nodded.

He continued, "And this Seed of Imagination is a beautiful flower with the colors of a magical night?"

We again nodded.

He continued. "Some time ago, a person with that description walked by, carrying a flower. I remember because I had never seen such a flower." He then spoke more quietly. "He was mean. He saw me carrying all my juggling equipment and purposely bumped into me, making me drop everything."

"Aaargh! That's him. I hate that magician!" said Kaia.

"Hold on," Alex the juggler continued. "He was really annoyed, and he kept repeating a phrase over and over again. It caught my attention, because it was a riddle, and I couldn't figure it out."

I rolled my eyes when he mentioned the riddle. What it is with riddles that get people so caught up in them?

"It's him, I'm sure it's him," said Kaia excitedly. "What was he saying?"

He took a few steps, trying to take his mind back to that moment in time and remember every word. "Hmmmm." He paused, took in some air, opened his eyes wider, pointed out with his index finger and when we were ready to hear it, he put his finger to his temple, thinking, and exhaled with another "hmmm." Really. He took another couple of steps and repeated it. When I thought I couldn't take it any longer, he finally smiled and exclaimed, "I got it, I remember!"

"Tell us, tell us!" we both said.

"The flower I will take with me
far away from those three.
And those two kids will never know
that in the darkness,
this seed will grow no more."

The only thing I could think was *why* a riddle, but Kaia sat down on the edge of the dock to think. I sat next to her, and thought. Alex joined in, sat next to me, and thought with us. "Hmmmm," the three of us said, as we put our index finger to our temples and tilted our heads slightly. "Hmmmmm," we repeated in unison, switching hands and tilting our heads in the opposite direction (apparently this made us think better).

"Where is he taking our flower?" I asked.

Suddenly bright-eyed Kaia said, "to a place where there is no light at all! But where?"

I then remember the scariest and darkest place told by different tales, and said, "The Drummer's Cave sure is dark."

"That's it, the Drummer's Cave!" exclaimed Kaia.

We still had the doubt of "those three," but that could be solved later. Right now we needed to find the flower. We thanked Alex, and walked back to our ship. We set sail and said goodbye. Alex wished us good luck, and almost ordered us to find the flower, because a world without imagination, would not be a fun place to be in. "Imagination should never be extinct," he said loudly with a final wave. We waved back until we couldn't see Alex anymore. And then we couldn't see the dock anymore. And then the only thing we could see were the stars shining above us.

Chapter 3
Discussion Questions

1. People with ASD find eye contact very difficult, and it is helpful to them to follow certain instructions or rules for common things such as a hand-shake.

2. Do you have something that you are passionate about?

3. Risho went through a meltdown, which is an emotional avalanche. They can happen at any time, and can be caused by a number of things such as environmental stimuli, stress, uncertainty and rapid changes.

4. What do you think Kaia's life is like having a brother in the spectrum? Try to think of both the good and the challenging.

5. Have you met anyone who is autistic?

6. What do you think a world without imagination would be like?

THE SADDEST CLOWN: LOVING AND ACCEPTING WHO YOU ARE

We now knew where to go, without knowing how to get there. It didn't matter to me, we would find a way. For the first time we start to enjoy our ship and I can smell the sweetness of its wood. I can see my sister smiling, closing her eyes and allowing the salty air to freshen up her face. The sound of the water breaking with our ship plays a smooth melody and my heart is happy.

We talk and eat delicious fresh fruit that Alex gave us for our trip, and sweet juicy mango drips from my cheeks. Normally, I would have never let that happen, but right now it felt different. I was being held by the universe. The dark sky felt like one of my blankets and I was wrapped tightly, with the soothing white noise from the ocean, like a baby inside a mother's womb. So nice, so safe. Besides, the taste of the mango I was eating was out of this world! Of course I did have a napkin with me so I cleaned every single drip along my mouth.

Time passed. How long? I don't exactly know, but we were able to sleep and rest. After some time of pure darkness, on the horizon we saw a light. It seemed to be carving a path in the sea for us to follow. A lighthouse, showing us the way to land, so we started preparing the ship for its arrival.

With the help of the lighthouse we could see the dock, but as the minutes passed and we got closer to land, the sun also began to wake up and give life to the harbor. I made sure the ship was securely tight, checking it three times before leaving it anchored. We walked straight towards the market. All the different smells came rushing to me like a hurricane blending together as one, and my stomach began to grumble. Only a few blocks away were the colorful tents placed next to each other shading the food and the vendors from the morning sun. As we got closer to the market, other people did, too. I was being guided by the smell of freshly squeezed orange juice, but got interrupted by the smell of hand-made tortillas with cheese melting squiggling out of the quesadilla. I could hear the sizzle of the cheese and I sneezed when I caught a whiff of chiles being roasted.

It started to get too crowded, and the sound of the juicers all around me trying to get every single drop of the orange in all the different stands was piercing. The sound managed to make its way into my brain, making it feel as if it were vibrating inside of me. I looked up as we walked towards the food stands, and saw the sun crashing on the many colorful tents that were shading us, although some rays still managed to make their way through in between each tent like a sword slicing through the fabric. Crowds of people were now walking near me, talking with one another, brushing against my arms without even noticing it. The high-pitched sound of laughter of two ladies standing in the corner echoed inside my head for the longest time. I forgot about how hungry I was, and my vision began to blur. I started to walk rapidly trying to find an exit from this endless tunnel of color. My strides became longer and faster until it became a full-out run to safety. I lifted my eyesight straight ahead, and I was able to see that there was an end to this market, so I ran even faster, bumping into people, barely noticing them or their stares and remarks about me. When I reached the end, I felt the cool morning breeze hit my face and was able to inhale the fresh salty air. It filled my lungs and calm washed over me. I walked towards the boardwalk, where I could hear the light hush of the crashing waves hit the wall over and over again. I sat, stared deep into the sea and waited for Kaia.

"Really?!" I heard Kaia after some time. "Really!?" she repeated, this time closer and definitely louder. She was upset. I knew it because her eye color had changed. Why was she upset? I'm the one who panicked.

"You can't just run out like that and leave me there every time you feel overwhelmed."

I had my eyes closed and was smiling, and hadn't heard a word she had said. I was focused on the sweet smell of the orange juice she had just brought. Delicious. Kaia smiled and extended her arm, giving me the best-tasting orange juice I had ever had and, you guessed it, no pulp! I just can't handle those tiny pieces swimming inside my mouth. I would rather not drink the juice at all. But this juice was exquisite.

Kaia also brought a plate of delicious quesadillas and sat next to me, legs swinging and taking in the view. Ahh, it was all good, until she said, "Did you notice something odd about this place?"

"Odd like how?" I asked with my mouth full of food.

"Well, odd...people are just..." she trailed off and didn't finish what she was saying. I was enjoying and savouring every taste of my breakfast and she kept quiet and pensive. "Risho," she said after a while, "something feels off."

She stood up and started walking towards the marketplace. I hesitated but caught up with her and walked next to her, feeling much better now that my belly was full. As we got closer, she whispered. "Look, do you see?"

As soon as she said it, I saw it. Everyone seemed to be in some sort of costume. Acrobats in tights, lion tamers with their whips, mimes, and clowns everywhere, some with full makeup, big red noses and happy smiles, others more conservative but still cheerful and laughing. Looking around we saw tent after tent of different circus performances. I wondered if Alex knew about this place; he would fit right in. We walked from one tent to another peeking in and saw people laughing and enjoying all kinds of different performances that were being put on stage. We left the tents and walked away from the crowds. We chose a narrow pebble street, and as we walked uphill, the sound of laughter faded in the distance. It was a beautiful place, the houses all painted in white, each with a different-colored rim. Kaia was still uncomfortable, still repeating that something was off, and kept looking back as if we were being followed.

Suddenly we heard someone crying, a sound that clashed completely with the laughter we had grown used to. It stopped us right in our tracks. We walked closer to where the sound was coming from. It came from a small alley right in the middle of the block. We stood right in the corner and listened again.

Yes, it was definitely crying. It was a clown, the saddest clown you have ever seen. "Why do you think that clown is so sad?" Kaia asked me.

The only thing I could think of was, why would Kaia think I would know? I mean that just didn't make sense at all, since we were both walking together and I knew as much as she did regarding the sad clown, so why? My thoughts were then interrupted by the sound of her voice. She had already walked over to the clown and was asking him what was wrong. The clown, still sobbing, just looked at her, lowered his gaze again and continued to cry. I walked over to them as Kaia sat down next to him. I copied her and sat on the other side of the clown. The alley was pretty dark, but it still had that wonderful smell of ocean spray and fresh flowers.

"What's wrong dear clown? Why are you so sad?" Kaia asked in a soft, tender voice.

The clown looked up again at her with hurt in his eyes, but this time he managed to say between sobs, "It's because someone took my smile from me." And then he continued crying.

"What do you mean someone took your smile," I asked, not understanding at all. You can't just grab a smile and take it with you; really, people should just speak clearer. It's so confusing.

"A really mean magician that I had never seen before was walking past me down by the boardwalk and took it!" He started crying again.

"Tell us more," Kaia said. "Maybe we can help."

"OK," the clown said and he slowly stood up. He was a small guy, smaller than I thought he would be, all dressed in black, and with a tiny red hat that matched his round red nose. The small amount of clown makeup he had was all smeared up by the tears. He started walking, narrating what had happened. "I was walking happily, greeting people with a big bright smile, it was such a beautiful day, and I was so happy to be a part of it. When suddenly, the meanest magician I had ever seen, with dark, evil eyes, started to laugh and to point at me. He kept saying things about my nose, about my clothes and then continued to make fun of my smile." The saddest clown took a deep breath and continued. "He then said, you are way too happy, and it irritates me, so I'm taking your smile." He said some magic words, and before I knew it he was gone and I was left like this." He pointed to himself and continued to cry. Kaia and I looked at each other, and Kaia's eye color began to change again. Oh no, I knew that look, and it meant trouble. Kaia's face began to turn red and I could see her hands turning into fists. She stood right up next to him and as controlled as she possibly could be, said "That's not right! The magician only does things that hurt others, we have to help him get his smile back," she said, looking at me. "I know it's him, the same evil magician that stole our Seed of Imagination. Listen, dear clown," she said authoritatively. "I really like your nose and also your clothes."

"I like your smile," I jumped in, "even if I don't see it now. But the most important and most beautiful thing to see in a person is a smile. Smiles make me happy."

"Yes," continued Kaia, "especially on a clown. It's part of who you are. Your smile brings happiness to children and you are capable of making everyone laugh. What a cool thing to do!"

I could see how the clown started to change his posture. He stood straighter, lifted his head and asked, "Do you really think so?"

"Of course!" we both said.

"Besides," Kaia went on, "you can't take someone like the magician seriously. He's mean and the only thing he does is bully people. You shouldn't believe him."

The clown lowered his eyes and I could feel him thinking. After a few moments he lifted his gaze and I saw a hint of sparkle in his eyes. He then affirmed, "I do like my smile, my nose and my clothes because they are a part of who I am."

Kaia continued, "That's right! You are a clown, totally unique and there will never be anyone like you."

The clown beamed, he flashed the biggest and brightest smile I have ever seen and that made me smile as well. "You gave me back my smile. How can I thank you?" he asked sincerely.

"Well, we are a bit tired, so it would be wonderful if we laughed and had some fun. When is you're next show?"

The clown looked at the time. "Come on! We have to run. I'll be late for the show. Follow me."

We ran out from the alley onto the pebbled street into the ever-so-bright sunlight that hurt my eyes, making me stop to close them while they continued to run. I finally caught up with them and ran down the pebbled street, passed the flower market, went through the colorful tents and out until we reached the circus tent.

Our friend the clown went through the back to get ready while we found two seats with a perfect view of the circus stage.

We returned to our places with popcorn and cotton candy. I couldn't decide which one to start eating first, so I went with both—that's right, alternating between the saltiness of the popcorn and the cloudlike sweet taste of the cotton candy that dissolved quickly in my mouth.

My taste buds were exploding when the lights inside the tent dimmed. Not knowing if it was day or night, this took us to a place where everything and anything could happen. The tent was then filled with music and everyone clapped to the rhythm in unison. Then, we all exploded with cheer as the clowns came out on stage. We immediately spotted our new friend. He was so funny and I could see the smile on everyone's face during his performance. I relaxed into my seat and enjoyed every moment of the show, listening to Kaia's laughter every now and then.

When the show ended, as we waited for the clown to come out so we could say goodbye to him, I reminded Kaia that we had to set sail soon in order to continue our search for the Drummer's Cave. It was clear that it wasn't in this port.

"Did I just hear you mention the Drummer's Cave?" the clown said to me as he came out of the dressing room and walked closer to us.

"Yes, the magician is taking our flower there, so it can grow no more." Kaia explained our quest to him.

"But we don't know how to get there," I continued.

"I remember the magician repeating a riddle over and over again," said the clown.

"What was it?" my sister asked hopefully. "What did he say?"

"Oh I remember it as clear as day:"

" I will soon arrive there
To the Drummer's Cave is where
But from her I will hide
She must not see me go inside
I will then have all the power
When I finally hide this flower."

"Who is 'her'?" I asked. Kaia was thinking, so I waited. Kaia turned to me with a wicked smile and a hint of amusement in her eyes "The magician has always been afraid and even respectful of only one name. Melia."

Literally my jaw dropped. "That's right!" I said, laughing. "But where does she live?"

We looked at each other. "She's the one who always finds us," stated Kaia.

Well not this time, I thought, we will find her, she can help us.

Kaia got closer to the clown, giving him an unexpected hug, and she then said to him, "Thank you, you have helped us so much. We will find Melia. I know we will. Remember to keep smiling so that your heart is happy. Don't let anyone hurt you like that again and much less take your smile away from you."

"Never again" is the only thing he managed to respond.

As we headed back to the dock, I kept seeing Kaia turning and looking back.

"Stop it," I said to her.

She slowly turned to me, her face pale, wide eyes, and said, "I think I just saw him."

Chapter 4
Discussion Questions

1. Risho tried to leave the market because it was too overwhelming with sound, people and visual stimuli. What do you think might have happened if he had stayed?

2. Usually family members and good friends can detect signs of a meltdown just about to happen before the kid even knows it. If you see these signs in your friend, it is best to take him/her away from that place to a quieter area.

3. Some autistic children tend to wander off, and that can be dangerous, so they carry trackers linked to family members and even the police to help keep them safe.

4. Everyone is unique! Love and embrace who you are, and never compare yourself to others.

5. List five great things about yourself.

6. No one has the power or the right to make you feel bad about your wonderful self. If you feel you are being emotionally abused by someone, tell a parent or a trusted adult.

5

LOST: THE DRAGON'S ROAR

K aia rushed me to our ship, face still pale as if she had seen a ghost—or worse, the magician. "What happened?" I pressured her into telling me.

"I don't know, I just had this feeling all along that we were being watched all the time, all of our moves." She paused, remembering our walk down the narrow streets when she felt a shadow moving; and then, while we were laughing during the show, a pair of eyes fixed on us.

"When we were saying goodbye to the clown," she continued, "I saw him. Believe me, it's true."

I believed my sister. I believed everyone—every word people said.

"Please, let's get out of here," my sister begged.

Once we were safe on the ship, she turned to ask me where we were going. I honestly had no clue...the day had gone by and the sun was beginning to set. I looked around for any kind of clue, but I couldn't seem to find any sort of guidance. Kaia's panic evolved into anger, and she accusingly told me that I had no idea where we were going. Even though she was right, I wasn't going to let her know that.

"You have no idea where to go!" she exclaimed.

"Of course I do!" I said with confidence as a mask. I kept sailing without any direction, looking around for any sort of clue, completely overwhelmed by the possibilities of knowing that each and every path would take me to a different outcome. Which direction should I choose?

Kaia's eyes began to change color, silently letting me know of her annoyance with me.

"We will head towards the West," I said. "And the moment the sun caresses the ocean, we will for sure have found Melia, and she will be able to help us."

We sailed and sailed towards the sun, and as it began to descend closer to the ocean for its night's rest, the beating of my heart became stronger, louder and faster. Dark gray clouds began to take over the beautiful melting colors of orange, red and pink, bringing a chill down my spine. The winds began to whistle loudly, slapping the ship's sails. How many times could the sails take that sort of beating without breaking?

A deep loud grumble of thunder vibrated throughout the gray ocean, bringing in heavy clouds full of water waiting to be dumped on us. A heavy fog built around us, but I had already detected a small boat that was trailing us, which made a sudden sharp turn in a direction away from the dark clouds. That same uneasy feeling in the pit of my stomach came back, and I believe I again heard the sound of trumpets mocking and teasing me.

"I told you! You have no idea where we are! We can't see the sun, we can't see anything at all with all this fog!" Kaia's voice was full of fear. "We're lost," she continued.

As soon as I heard that, I was the one who lost it. I couldn't handle her feeling that way, and snapped. I said in defense, "At least I'm trying, but the only thing you do is complain."

Tears stung her eyes, and she snapped right back at me telling me how all of this was my fault, how I let the magician take our flower from us.

I didn't even know the Seed of Imagination was missing from our room. I think that is what saddened me the most. How can something so important be taken from right under our nose and we don't even know it? This time literally, taken from right under our nose, because sometimes these sayings have no meaning at all in my opinion, like "It's raining cats and dogs" or "You're driving me up the wall." So confusing! But this, this was literal.

"If you would've watered it as you said you would, you would have known it was missing, so stop blaming me." shouted Kaia.

We kept saying things to each other back and forth while the fog took over, surrounding everything, the wind constantly mingling in our conversation and even some raindrops were starting to fall. We hadn't even realized that the ship had docked on a stranded beach. "It was our responsibility," emphasized Kaia, "plus, you're not even interested anymore. You ignore everyone all the time and want to be left alone in your room. Well, I'll leave you alone." Realizing we were on shore, she got out the ship and started to walk down the beach.

I immediately went after her. I enjoyed her company and being with her; it's just that sometimes I can get too caught up in my own thinking and don't even know how much time has passed being all by myself. Sometimes, the things in my head are simply more interesting than when I connect to what's going on outside.

Rain started pouring down heavily, and I was finally able to catch up with her. When I did, there was a blinding light that illuminated the whole island, followed by the deafening sound of thunder. Instinctively, Kaia screamed.

"It's only thunder," I explained. "It's alright."

I could see calm wash over her face, when suddenly, the earth shook with a loud roar. Her eyes widened and her natural flow of breathing stopped for a second.

"What was that?" I asked to the air. The earth under my feet rumbled when the second deep roar was heard again. "It sounds like...." Logic stopped my sister's train of thought. She continued, "No, it can't be, we're too far out."

"Are you thinking the same thing I am?" I asked.

Kaia nodded, and together we exclaimed, "The dragon!"

"But how?" she asked. "He never flies this far out."

I thought the same thing she did, not understanding how he could be all the way out of his zone, when on the horizon, out of the heavy gray fog and the curtain of rain, a glimmer of what looked like a shiny armor lit the darkness. It was as if a purple spotlight had been turned on. It became bigger with every passing second, the bright purple light taking shape, as the heavy flapping of the wings brought gusts of wind in a rhythmic pattern shaking the trees .As it got closer I could see how the scales that resembled his armor had all kinds of different colors, from a dark burgundy to the lightest of blues.

He flew straight towards us, fierce. He was aware of his grandeur and strength, a confidence that I admired. We were paralyzed under the thunderstorm, looking up as rain fell on our faces just watching this majestic creature charge towards us. As he got closer, I could see the fire that burnt behind his eyes, his roar building again from deep inside of him.

"Watch out!" I yelled just in time for us to be able to duck as the dragon flew past just above us with a deafening roar that shook the earth's core once more. He continued the trajectory of his flight and slowly disappeared, his purple light dimming as he flew into the curtain of water behind us.

Once we were sure he was gone, we slowly got back on our feet, soaking wet. I did not know if it was fear or the cold, but my body shook uncontrollably.

"Risho." I heard my sister softly say my name. "I got really scared."

"Me too," I said. There was no denying it. "What was the dragon doing all the way out here?" I asked the same question again.

"Let's focus on the flower for now," said my sister. "We'll find out later what the dragon was doing here." My sister had a mission, and it was to find the Seed of Imagination.

The rain had gotten lighter, the fog was lifting and you could even see again some blue patches that belonged to the sky. She started to walk, leaving me behind, but after a few steps, she paused, turned and walked straight to me. Without warning, she gave me a hug, which made my body tense and back up.

I've been told hugs make people feel good. I don't like them, but I do know they come out of love, and that is what makes me feel good regardless of the invasion of my personal space. She then held my hand, knowing I don't like that either, and told me how sorry she was for getting upset. I pulled my hand away, and she then went into explaining how she felt sad and angry for losing the flower mom had given us, and how nervous she was thinking that we might not ever get it back. I also told her I was sorry. Although I couldn't pinpoint what I was feeling I did know it was a feeling I did not like.

"We will find it," I said, and she agreed by nodding her head.

"You know what?" Kaia said. "We are brother and sister, and we shouldn't fight."

"I know," I said.

"We take care and support one another," she added, repeating the exact words my mom often says to us. Kaia continued: "You know what else we are the champions of? Having fun!" And just like that, my sister tagged me and called out, "You're it!" She started sprinting into the woods because she knew I was coming to get her. She's super-fast and agile, so she zig-zagged through trees, ducked under the heavy branches full of leaves and splashed on puddles, laughing every time she did.

I was having fun too, and lost focus of what or who I was chasing. I hummed away, letting the sound fill my ears, and skipped behind my sister. I felt happy, the humid earthy scent of the mud engulfed me, and my senses sharpened as everything around me moved at a slower pace. I could see the details of every single raindrop as they clung to the leaves while the branches were being sharply pushed to one side in order for me to pass by. I saw how a single raindrop full of incomparable beauty lost its grip and fell, reflecting light, allowing itself to shine brightly. It landed on a leaf, and then respectfully continued its route, gracing the leaf as it slid down to its end, to make the final plunge to the ground, enjoying every moment of that freedom during the fall before meeting the others at the end of their journey in the puddle on the ground.

Then, like a broken spell, time returned back to its usual and normal pace, and I continued running, skipping, laughing, tagging each other while the clouds moved on, and the young night sky was revealed. Kaia started going deeper within the woods. That made me anxious and I called out to her.

"Hold on," she said loudly enough for me to hear her over the new sounds of the woods.

"Kaia!" I repeated, not wanting to follow.

"I saw something," she said loudly. "Just give me a minute."

Of course I started counting the seconds with a perfect and steady spacing between one second and the next. "Fifty-eight, fifty-nine, sixty! That's one minute, Kaia!" I said from the top of my lungs, so she could hear me while I looked out to try and see her.

She popped out right in front of me with a huge smile. "I'm here!"

Aaaargh!!!! She gave me a huge scare! "Stop scaring me!"

Kaia laughed. She knows I hate being pranked and scared like that, and she does it repeatedly.

"It's not funny! It never is," I repeated for at least the hundredth time.

"Look what I found." She pulled out from behind her back one of our flower's petals. My eyes rose from the petal to her eyes, and she continued. "It's another one of our petals. I think the dragon dropped it as he flew straight through here." Kaia pulled out the other petal from her bag and compared both of them. It was undoubtedly from our flower.

"Why was the dragon carrying one of our petals?" I asked.

"I don't know," responded Kaia, her voice tense and deep in thought, trying to figure this whole thing out.

"We have to find Melia," I said. "We need her help."

Chapter 5
Discussion Questions

1. Playful jokes and sayings are hard for children in the spectrum to understand, since they take everything so literally. When talking to a friend in the spectrum, try to use direct language.

2. Some autistic children have a strong bond with a parent, guardian or family member, and might feel very strongly what the other person is feeling without being able to distinguish or separate that the emotion belongs to someone else. That happened at the beginning of this chapter when Kaia's emotions became his as well.

3. Autistic children have a difficult time describing and understanding their emotions. Do you know what triggers different emotions in yourself? Try and name a few emotions and what makes you feel that way.

6

MELIA, KEEPER
OF THE WOODS

e walked deeper into the woods. We stopped playing and talking altogether, but we weren't in complete silence; in fact, I think that at that particular time, there was even more chattering, but not by us. So many unidentified sounds filled the air, it seemed that crickets were announcing our arrival, while other bigger, but hidden animals gossiped about us. The light changed again, to softer, warmer tones, making me feel more welcomed here. I could see Kaia gazing up at the huge trees that provide us with life. We walked in deeper still, the trees getting taller and the foliage more intense around us, trapping us in a tight earthly hug.

Kaia was guiding the way. We moved slower, fighting our way through the vines that were keeping us close together. My sister lifted an enormous leaf, went under it, and made her way through. Then I heard her quiet gasp as she held her breath for a split second. I pushed her a little to the side since she hadn't moved an inch, and I was left crouching under the leaf, unable to move either backwards or forward.

"Kaia, move," I said.

She took a single step to the left, which made it possible for me to emerge from where I was. As I took that step forward and lifted my eyes, I understood why it took her breath away. The forest had a clearing in the shape of a circular stage. Deep brown tree roots came out from the earth re-creating a bench. All sorts of wildflowers were perfectly distributed around it, giving splashes of color and untamed beauty to the green foliage that surrounded us. It smelled so fresh and delicious, I wanted to bottle up the scent of the woods and take it home with me.

On the other side of the clearing was a thick patch of soft moss nestled by tree branches that resembled a bed. Above it was a perfectly cut out circle like a telescope, where you could clearly see the night sky. The stars shone clear and bright and the moonlight entered through there just like a spotlight illuminated a superstar. And then, there she was, as beautiful as ever: Melia.

She is not easy to find, but she taught us well and we were able to spot her. Her gown is made of leaves and earthly elements that change with the seasons, and are woven together to make her blend into the woods. Flowers and the thinnest of vines were braided in her long, thick brown hair, making it difficult to distinguish from a tree trunk. She was dancing. We were unable to move, watching how elegantly and smoothly she danced across the stage nature provided her with, leaping and turning with the wind. She then, with one hand, held a vine from the tallest tree and with her touch, melted it into the smoothest, chocolate-colored silk. She wrapped her bare foot around it and effortlessly pulled herself up.

Then, I completely lost sight of her for a second as she blended completely into the background, making herself one with the tree. But there she was again, wrapping herself with the silk at the highest point of the tree like a butterfly cocoon all tucked in. In a blink of an eye she let go, completely unwrapping herself, spinning faster and faster towards the ground, giggling all the time as she spun down only to be caught at the end by the silk that was holding her from the waist only inches from the grass. She untied the silk from her waist and held on to it, still wearing a huge smile on her face, and she swung again and gave one more twirl that ended up with her staring right at us.

She froze when she realized she had two pairs of eyes watching her every move. She tugged hard on the silken vine and vanished into the tree top like a rocket being launched into space. Before we knew it, I heard the melody of her voice next to us. "Risho and Kaia." The sound of our names coming from her voice was warm and gentle with a sprinkle of surprise. We didn't dare move, not knowing how she was going to react; but then she opened her arms, prompting us to give her a hug.

Kaia rushed to her and held her in a tight embrace. At that moment, we knew everything was going to be just fine.

"I haven't seen you children in so long. I've missed you." She took a step back and looked us over from head to toe. "You've grown so much," Melia said in a nostalgic tone.

"We've missed you too, so much," Kaia said for both of us. I went straight to the point and told her we needed her help.

"Tell me everything," she said.

"It's the magician. He stole our flower."

"Yes," Melia whispered, lowering her eyes. "I heard something like that had happened."

"How did you know?" Kaia couldn't hide the surprise in her tone.

"The dragon told me."

"The dragon?!" I blurted out, like I usually did when things didn't make sense to me. "We just saw him!

"In fact," Kaia said opening her bag and getting one of the petals out, "he just dropped this." Kaia extended her arm and gave the petal to Melia.

"Why did he have a petal from our flower?" I asked, starting to run out of patience. But Melia tenderly took the petal in her hand, which glowed slightly with her touch. She smiled at it and said "Your flower, I remember it very well. I was there when your mother gave it to you—did you know that?"

We both silently nodded, and she continued. "The magician was there, too."

Now that was unexpected. Our surprised expression gave way for Melia to continue to explain. "He's always wanted that flower for himself, and many times had tried to steal it unsuccessfully, because you had never let him before. You were always too close to it, taking care of it, watering it, or simply just taking in its beauty. Until one day, you completely forgot you had that valuable gift, and he didn't hesitate to take it from you." She paused, remembering that day, took a cleansing breath and continued. "I tried to stop him. You know I am always there for both of you, but on that day, he was faster than me."

"And the dragon?" I still didn't understand where the dragon fit into all of this.

"When he found out that the Seed of Imagination was in the magician's hands, he knew darkness would come, and he's been trying to recover it since."

"The Seed of Imagination must be very important, then," Kaia said, not realizing until now its great value.

"You have no idea, my sweet child," Melia said, and continued to explain. "Imagination is the seed of knowledge and a great sign of intelligence. For this and other reasons, it is cherished, valued and sought by many. It is a gift that many would go to great lengths to have. I sincerely hope you are able to recover it and take it back home."

"That's why we're here," I said, "and we know where it is."

"Yes, but we don't know how to get there," Kaia added.

"Where is it?" Melia asked.

"The Drummer's Cave," we both responded.

When Melia heard the name, she tried to hide from us the fear in her eyes. "Are you sure?" was the only thing she managed to ask.

We nodded, and she took my sister by the hand, guiding us to the bench. We sat down, and she said, "Tell me everything you know, so I can help you get it back safely."

We told her everything. The ship, the riddles, the places we'd been, our new friends and how we had been followed. Melia explained to us why the boat that was trailing us here wasn't able to follow us any farther than the point where it changed directions. "My land has an ancient wisdom of the purest kind, and anything that is dark and evil is unable to get through."

"Like a protection bubble?" asked Kaia.

"Yes, something like that. While you're here you're completely safe, but be careful as soon as you leave, because we can't protect you outside the woods, and he will do everything in his power to prevent you from taking back that flower. Rest now and gain your strength back. You will need it."

We feasted on delicious food from the forest that nurtured our bodies, and then curled up in the cozy moss bed for the night. I could feel all the animals in the forest guarding us as I drifted off to sleep.

At sunrise, Kaia was already awake. Around her were all the animals of the forest, from the biggest to the smallest, laughing and talking. Kaia likes to talk, and apparently she found her crowd. When she heard me getting closer she turned with a huge grin. She has always been an animal lover, so I knew that this moment was a happy and memorable one. After breakfast, Melia took us around the island, and we decided to spend most of the day at the beach, recovering from the previous days and gaining strength for what awaited us at the Drummer's Cave.

We played for hours with the waves, jumping over them and going under, gathering the pure white foam that was remainder of the wave that had just crashed down. We made sand castles, many of them, with towers and bridges, with protective walls and ditches. During sunset, I stood at that point on the beach where the waves stretch the farthest, trying to reach me and tickle my toes. One hand on my waist, my gaze was completely lost in that place where the horizon and the sea meet. There was a blurred space right there that always seemed to call me; it felt like the song of dolphins speaking to me.

"Risho has been standing there for some time," Melia said to Kaia.

"Yes, he does that. Everytime we go to the beach, at some point he will just stay there, so still, looking out. I can never figure out what he's thinking and he will never say. I actually don't even think he knows, but his eyes say otherwise. There's so much depth in them." Melia came closer to me and stood right next to me, looking out, following my line of sight.

"Beautiful, right?" Melia said.

I simply turned and said, "I'm hungry. Let's go."

And just like that, our day at the beach was over.

When the sky changed from orange to pink and purple, we prepared our things and got ready to leave. Melia walked with us to the ship, and made sure everything was ready for us to continue.

"You are very close now to the Drummer's Cave. It's dark now and it's a beautiful clear sky, so it should be easy getting there. Follow your heart, and the stars will guide you."

As she said goodbye to us, Melia felt uneasy, even though the mermaid at the bow gleamed and gave her a reassuring wink of the eye. Melia knew we were protected by the mermaid in the ocean, but it was what could happen on land, once we reached the Drummer's Cave, that worried her.

We set sail towards the Drummer's Cave. "OK, Kaia, get out the map," I said.

"What map?" she asked.

"Really, Kaia...the map Melia gave you to the Drummer's Cave," I said, not understanding my sister's lack of common sense.

"Risho, there's no map. You were there when she said to both of us that the stars would guide us."

"Are you kidding me!" was my only thought, but I stayed silent.

We looked up and saw thousands of bright stars shining all jumbled in no particular order. I looked up again and they had changed, both in shape and brightness. I felt that familiar but unwelcome feeling building inside of me. I tried to breathe deeply, but the high humidity of the air was oppressing and I couldn't breathe. I sat down to calm myself. Kaia repeated the words spoken by Melia: "Follow your heart and the stars will guide you."

"What does that even mean?!" I exclaimed furiously.

Again Kaia was trying to make sense out of this, but she needed to hurry, because the ship was drifting in no particular direction, night-time was here, we knew we were being followed and this time, we had no protection. I was no help at all at that particular moment. I sat on the floor of the wooden ship, trying to breathe deeply and looking at Kaia. I was relying on her.

Chapter 6
Discussion Questions

1. Children with autism tend to blurt out what they're thinking without realizing if it's appropriate or not. Can you share something you have wanted to say but couldn't because it was socially inappropriate? Why do you think or know it was not the right time to express what you were thinking?

2. Why do you think imagination is so important?

3. Sometimes it is hard to have a conversation with a child with autism, or even to get an answer that makes sense to the question you asked. Try and talk with an autistic boy or girl. Even though you might not get a full conversation or even a straight answer, it will make a difference to them in their day.

7

THE DRUMMER'S CAVE: CONQUERING YOUR FEARS

Kaia could feel my stare and she knew it was up to her to figure out how to get to the Drummer's Cave. She seemed calm regarding what was at stake. Without saying a word, she went to the bow of the ship and sat down, closed her eyes, and let the hot night breeze clear her thoughts. After a couple of minutes, Kaia finally opened her eyes. I had been staring at her like a hawk, and she was finally ready to speak. She moistened her lips, clearing the sea salt that clung to them, and said, "Risho, we need to do this together. Please come and sit next to me."

I didn't want to move. I couldn't. I was paralyzed with fear.

"I know you can," encouraged my sister. "Stand up," she ordered.

I did. My legs wobbled like a newborn calf and I felt dizzy.

"Breathe in and out," she continued.

I obeyed.

"Now walk four steps towards me."

I counted the steps out loud. That had always helped me in the past. "One" step "two" step "three" step "four" step. I was right there next to my sister, her hand stretched out for me to hold.

"You're going to love this, it feels like a ride on the roller-coaster" she said with a smile. "Sit next to me."

I sat down at the very end of the ship's bow, and when I looked up the feeling was amazing. I felt as if I were flying on top of the ocean, the sound of the ship splitting the water, and no other sound was heard. It was magical, I felt something shift inside of me, calm surrounded us and I could again hear the song of the dolphins.

"Follow your heart," they whispered, repeating Melia's words.

I didn't know exactly what that meant, but I did know that at that point I was happy, with the air on my face, the feeling of flight over the ocean and the sound of the dolphins whispering in my ear. I closed my eyes to take it all in, and when I opened them, I looked up again at the black curtain above us. Some stars were so much brighter than others—twinkling, trying to get my attention. How could I have missed it before? It was so clear now, in every direction, pattern after pattern of clues, one after another—they were everywhere, guiding us. It was the map we needed to the Drummer's Cave. I could feel Kaia smiling. She knew I could now see the map above us.

We knew where we were going and how to get there. The mermaid gleamed, announcing our presence, illuminating the way in the vast sea, and there was no trace at all that we were being followed. It felt good, we were happy to finally being able to reach our destination, as dangerous as it might be.

I looked up at the map. "We should be getting close by now," I announced.

Kaia nodded in agreement.

I cut the engine and continued only with the help of the hushed wind blowing on the sails. We moved slowly and in complete silence, until there it was... A chill ran down my spine and goosebumps warned me of what was coming. Kaia's eyes widened when we heard the very first thumping of a faint drum coming from afar. We were here.

We hid the ship as best as we could and walked towards the very faint and light sound of the beating drums, almost intertwining with my own heartbeat. The night was very still. We closely watched every step we took, probably being too careful just in order to take more time in reaching the cave, but still every step got us closer. The sound of the beating drums thumped more deeply in our core, making the blood in our veins shake with every thumping as we got closer. We finally saw a faint light and stopped, hiding in the dense jungle, where we felt somewhat safe. With every beat of the drum the leaves shook as well, giving this whole place a single heartbeat. Spying from behind some trees, Kaia whispered "I can see a torch next to the entrance of the cave. It seems no one is here."

"What do you mean no one is here?"

"I mean, no one is here."

"Well, someone must be here, it's not like they're just going to leave everything unguarded."

"I know! I mean, I can't see anyone!" Kaia said through clenched teeth.

"Really Kaia," I said. "It's so confusing, you should speak more...."

She cut me off mid-sentence with daggers in her eyes, and in a very, very clear and quiet voice she said, "S t o p i t n o w, we can talk about how properly I speak later, at home, OK?"

"OK," I answered. It sounded fair enough given the circumstances. "I'm a bit hungry, though," I informed her, while spying the entrance of the cave. Kaia turned to me rubbing her face in exasperation. I took out the granola bar that I carry with me, ripped the paper and took a bite. Mmmm it was so good. I hadn't realized how hungry I got when I was nervous. While eating my savory treat, Kaia looked at me with that look that made her eye color change.

"Sorry" I said, with my mouth full, "I couldn't find the chewy kind..."

Kaia rolled her eyes and sat down, waiting for me to finish my snack, clenching her jaw with every crunch-filled bite I took.

There. I felt much better. I crumpled the paper—not very quietly, I have to admit—and then tiptoed around.

"What are you doing?" asked Kaia quietly.

"Looking for a trash can."

Kaia was next to me in an instant. She gave me one of those looks I don't understand, and snatched the wrapper from me, shoving it in her pocket. "Now, let's continue," she hissed without looking back at me.

Asking her for some water I thought would be inappropriate, so I kept quiet and followed her. We came out of our hiding place and walked towards the cave, looking around, making sure no one could see us. I heard some rustling leaves nearby and gave a light, very light yelp.

"Be quiet," Kaia said.

"I heard something," I answered her, still being as quiet as possible. "Maybe it was the same person that was following us," I continued, "or maybe it's just an animal passing by."

She answered back at me with "Hmm." Well that made more sense than my theory of being followed, so we made our way to the cave's entrance.

Everything was very still. A torch illuminated the cave's dark mouth, welcoming us in. Once we took a step inside, the moment our foot crossed the threshold, a series of torches lit one by one illuminated a long, narrow tunnel. We walked down the tunnel without being able to see the end of it, the walls of the cave starting to drip sweat from above letting us know we were going further underground. It was very humid and hot, our own sweat was getting into our eyes, and we had to constantly wipe it off. The sound of the drums was getting louder and faster, mimicking the beating of our own hearts. The flames from the torches danced away to the rhythm of the drums, giving movement to the tunnel walls while painting it in different tones of red and orange. We finally reached the end of the narrow tunnel, where it opened up into a very wide and round space, almost like a sphere. Its ceiling was much higher with a dome-like shape, surrounded by the many other tunnels that joined here. It was as if we had been crawling up a spider's leg and we had reached its body.

"There!" Kaia pointed to the center of the circle, where our flower stood alone, still glowing with the strength of a million stars inside it. The stem had angled a bit trying to nurture itself from the only crack in the ceiling where a faint beam of moonlight made its way through, reaching its petals, giving it hope. The flower's own light dulled our sight, and couldn't fully see what was at the entrance of the rest of the tunnels that joined here forming a circle guarding the Seed of Imagination.

When at last our eyes adjusted, we saw them. Four men with loose black pants, their torsos fully marked with symbols in black ink, and there, standing in front of each man were their drums. The drums were actually beautiful, dark deep blue and black, so shiny that they reflected the symbols they had on their bodies. The rims were silver, and looked old and worn out, with carvings engraved, each set with a different pattern. They seemed to be playing in a trance, to a steady beat, their faces without any sort of expression, not aware of their surroundings.

Kaia left the safety of the darkness in the tunnel and tried to make her way to the center to get our flower, but as soon as she took that first step, I fiercely pulled her back, grabbing her arm.

"What do you think you're doing?" I asked her nervously.

"Getting the flower, it's right there and there's no one around."

"No one around? Are you kidding me?" I looked straight at the tall, well-built men drumming away.

"They don't even know we're here," she said. "They're in a trance."

We found a pebble and threw it at one of the drummer's feet, just to double-check our theory of them being in a trance. Nothing, not a muscle flinched. Kaia was ready to go in, but I stopped her again.

"What if it's a trap?" I said.

"But there's no one," she responded, looking around once more, just making sure.

"Very well, let's do this together."

We very slowly made our way to the center of the dome where our flower stood, constantly looking around us. The drummers were completely still like carved marble sculptures, with only their arms moving in order to create the thumping of the drums. We circled the flower very slowly, making sure it was clear of anything and it was safe for us to grab. Kaia and I were facing each other with the flower between us, then she mouthed "one, two, three," and we slowly reached for it and picked it up.

The instant we touched it, the fire at the entrance of every tunnel intensified, the hollow drummer's eyes pinned us and their hands began moving to a completely different rhythm, announcing our arrival. It was fast, loud and very deep, their eyes so dark and intense drilling into us. The sound became some sort of a spell, and we couldn't move. The beating echoed in the cave, and from two of the tunnels opposite from each other, two beautiful female dancers were spat out from them, and made a circle around us. Their bodies moved to the rhythm of the drums in a primal dance, and they locked their eyes with ours. They too had their bodies covered with the same symbols as the drummers.

The beating of the drums was so intense and deafening, I could feel a raw and wild instinct building deep in my core.

From the tunnel behind us another dancer shot out, this time a male. He could maneuver and bend fire as he pleased; it danced all around him flipping and turning as he too circled around us, creating a wall of fire that moved to the beat of the drums. The drumming was now faster and louder, and their movements became a blur, spinning and spinning around us, making me dizzy. In came another man with the same loose black pants and more of those black symbols painted all over his body. He jumped, turned and moved all around us as in a fight, a dance, or acrobatics. I was so dizzy and overwhelmed by the drumming, the dancing, the fire and now someone somersaulting over me that I had to reach into my pocket and hold on to my stone. Just feeling its cool smooth texture began to relax me enough to be able to see and hear more clearly.

My hand held onto the stone, but this time, something was different. I received energy or information from it. My eyes closed and everything quietened. I was inside an invisible bubble, muting every sound as if I was underwater. I opened my eyes, and turned slowly to face my sister. Kaia's eyes were wide with fear. A protective instinct rose from inside of me. The protective bubble expanded to cover her as well. As soon as it locked her in, her eye color went back to that beautiful golden honey and yellow amber. She closed her eyes and I saw how the air she took in expanding her lungs calmed her down. When she opened them, she turned to me and smiled. This didn't last very long, though. The sudden stop of the drumming and of all movement around us made me drop the stone in my pocket again. The cool, protective bubble popped and the hot air that surrounded us grabbed me by the throat, making it hard for me to take in a breath. A dark, low-pitched laughter filled the cave, getting closer and closer until I felt his presence. It was him. It was the magician.

Chapter 7
Discussion Questions

1. Have you ever felt in the pit of your stomach or your chest a feeling that you are doing something that "feels" right or even that "feels" wrong?

2. Risho is very good at seeing patterns. Name one thing you know you are good at. Now, be proud of it.

3. Kaia was very patient while Risho ate his granola bar. Have you ever been very patient with someone else, or has someone else been patient with you? What was the reason? Remember, everyone is different, and that doesn't make them more or less than you.

4. Have you ever faced something you're afraid of and then felt very proud about it? What was it?

THE DUEL: STRONGER THAN YOU THINK

"**W**here do you think you're taking that, boy?"

The sound of his voice triggered a memory that made the little hairs on the back of my neck raise in warning like cactus thorns.

"We came to get our flower that you stole from us." I tried to sound as confident as possible, probably not succeeding to its fullest.

Laughter filled the cave echoing around us. "And you thought you were just going to come in and take it from me, just like that?"

My sister couldn't keep quiet any longer. "It's ours!" she snapped back at him.

He turned and looked at her. She held his stare. He made way towards her and everyone's eyes followed. The acrobat somersaulted his way across the floor, guarding the magician's side landing inches from Kaia. The magician was now so close to her she could smell the awful stench coming from his mouth when he spoke again.

"Yes, little girl..." He gave her a slow, threatening smile, showing her his dark and rotten teeth. "But this flower...it has powers. Anyone who possesses the Seed of Imagination is capable of anything and everything." He paused, assessing his prey. "So, give it back!"

In a blink of an eye, he snatched the flower from our hands. The drumming began to thump so loud and fast that I had to cover my ears. Everyone moved so fast around me. In no time, the acrobat was again next to the magician, catching the flower that had been tossed to him. The acrobat jumped, taking it further away from us. The fire in the man's hands lit again, and ran around us in a circle. The dancers curved their bodies to every beat of the drum, and followed the trail of fire, taunting us with their moves.

Chaos within order. I could see the flower now being guarded by monkey man. I reached into my pocket to grab the stone, and felt the familiar calm rush to me with its touch. The cool protective bubble formed again. It blocked all external sound, and I could hear my own heart thumping, speaking to me. Everything seemed to be moving a lot slower. I took a deep breath, just as I was taught, so I could calm down, not letting go of my stone. I could feel its power building up traveling from my hand into my body.

I was never good at any kind of sports. I did try, though, but my body simply didn't react as coordinated as I would have liked, which usually meant that I was the last one to be picked for a team. That I did understand very clearly. The feeling of being unwanted hurt, and it made me just want to go home.

Loosening the grip on the stone, made the thumping aggressively come back punching my senses. I wanted to be home at that precise moment, in my bed, under the safety of all of my covers. Tears started welling in my eyes. It was too much, too much—I couldn't handle it. Taking in all of my surroundings, my eyes stopped at the sight of my sister fighting to recover our flower. Everyone was laughing at her, as she chased after it, the flower being tossed from one person to another. I had to help. I held on to the stone once again, and the power from it sparked something from within. I held it tight, feeding from its energy, and then I believed I could do it.

I took my hand out of my pocket without letting go of the stone, holding on to it very tightly. I let it guide my movements, my body. I came closer to the magician, hands on guard like I've seen people do when they're ready to fight. He was watching the whole choreography unfold before him, laughing, enjoying how Kaia was being taunted and mocked by everyone, the flower passing from one set of hands to another building her frustration. He had ignored me completely, knowing I was useless, just standing there not doing a single thing. Well surprise, I was standing right next to him, ready to fight. My hands were still up letting him know without a single word that I was ready to fight. He looked at me and laughed. This time, I didn't mind and held my head high, hands still up and ready. He charged towards me, and this time, I didn't close my eyes, didn't even flinch. My hands knew exactly what to do. I protected myself from all the punches thrown by the magician.

It was our turn to dance now. We made our way to the center of the circle, blocking kicks and punches that were being thrown. The drummers kept hitting and pounding on the drums furiously, the acrobat stood guarding the flower, and my sister was in between the two females, each one holding one of her arms. Everyone had their eyes pinned to the center, where the main fight was taking place. Again, he charged towards me. I instinctively blocked every single punch, and came back with some tricks of my own, taking me completely by surprise. Choreographed kicks and punches flew through the air, in a back-and-forth lethal dance. I stole a quick glance towards Kaia. Her mouth was open, unable to believe what she was seeing. I was even able to give her a little side grin, not believing it myself.

Fast and precise movements kept leaving my body when suddenly, from across the room, the acrobat tossed the magician a sword. It flew across the air, and right under the dome's crack, it caught a glimpse of moonlight. The slick metal shone for an instant, blinding me, and giving him an advantage that he didn't hesitate to take. He came to me sword in hand. I backed up and jumped on a pile of rocks, climbing them as slickly and as fast as I could, getting away from the sharp metal before me. There was no way out of this one. I jumped to the far end of the cave, getting away for an instant, knowing I would soon be pinned against the wall. The magician made his way towards me, taking his time, the drumming faster and stronger with each step that he took towards me. He was so close to me, I could see the sweat trickling down his forehead, his dark cape floating ever so slightly behind him with every step he took. His rotten smell told me he was now inches away from me. He laughed again, enjoying every moment of this.

The Seed of Imagination

"I have been waiting for a long time to put an end to the Seed of Imagination," he said, a dark laugh cascading out from him again. He swung his sword back to strike the flower from its roots when a familiar roar was heard, shaking the earth.

Everyone lost their balance as the floor shook and cracked from under our feet, and the ceiling from the dome above us began to crumble ever so slightly. Kaia covered her head from the falling rocks from above, and then, with a force of a million tons, something slammed right on the highest point of the dome, right where the thinnest of the cracks was, exactly where the flower was feeding itself from the slightest light that came through all the previous nights that it had been standing here on its own. With a last thud, the cave's dome shattered completely, pieces of earth falling like raindrops. The top of the dome was now decapitated and we could see the stars above us, and then, the spikes at the end of the dragon's tail rose again to strike down with all its might and destroy it for good.

"Stop!" the magician ordered. Everything paused for a second, the dragon's tail still lifted waiting for the order to strike down, and no one dared take in a breath, waiting for what was to come. And then I recognized her voice. "That is enough, do not touch a petal of that flower, or I'll shatter this place to pieces."

The magician recognized her voice, too, and trying to remain as calm as he could, disguising his anger, he said, "Show your face, Melia."

Kaia and I looked at each other from one side of the cave to the other. There was a faraway thunderous roar from the heavens that brought a refreshing breeze of cool air into the cave. I breathed it in deeply, my lungs ever so grateful for this. Everyone was looking up at the huge hole in the dome, clouds beginning to form in the night sky. Then the dragon's head was in view, peeking in to take a look inside, his eyes taking in everyone there.

"It's OK." I heard Melia's voice again. "Put me down."

The dragon's face got closer and closer to us as he leaned forward and down through the dome's hole, his face barely fitting through. One of his eyes was now so close, looking straight at me. His vertical pupil widened ever so slightly and I could see my reflection in it. His nostrils were inches from the magician, with a whiff taking in his stale smell, and huffing it out with disgust. I saw Kaia giggle at the dragon's disapproval.

Melia slid down the dragon's neck, unmounting him and landing right at the center of the cave. She gave the dragon a pat that sent him back to straighten up, unblocking the newly made hole from above us. He was still there though, on guard.

"Well well well, to what do I owe this honor?" the magician asked, giving a slight bow to Melia

"This has gone far enough"

"Whatever do you mean?" The magician took a step closer to her, keeping a grip on his sword

"You know this flower belongs to them. Give it back. Now" Melia's eyes had a certain strength I had seen before.

"But you see, I don't really want to.... I don't think that I will. And you know what? For centuries I've been tired of you, too..."

The fast hard beating of the drums began as soon as the magician without any warning charged with his sword toward Melia, not even giving her a chance at all to get out of the way.

The heavens and the dragon roared simultaneously as the magician's sword pierced Melia, and for a brief second, time stood still. The beating of the drums stopped, as everyone very quickly assessed what had just happened. What came next happened so fast. Everyone scattered down the multiple spider's legs hiding, bracing themselves for what was to come next, while Kaia and I rushed to Melia, who was now lying on the floor. The dragon roared again with pain and fury in his eyes, and the sky began to cry. Melia was able to smile faintly, and put her hand out, rejoicing in the drops of water landing on us.

"It's raining" she softly said, with a thin smile.

I, on the other hand, wasn't smiling at all, I was pretty much panicking.

Melia was about to speak again. Kaia and I leaned closer to be able to hear what she was about to say, when the magician came out of one of the spider's legs and peeked in through the remains of the dome where we were. He laughed, a cruel laughter that echoed all around.

I felt the blood in my body begin to boil in anger. I stood up, while my sister stayed with Melia. I didn't hesitate to charge to where he was standing, looking at us, laughing. When I tackled him, he completely vanished right from under my arms, leaving just a trace of colored dust in the air. Then, I heard him again, his laughter traveling from a different direction to my ears. I turned, and again saw him standing at the entrance of another one of spider's legs. I ran towards him again, crossing to the other end of the dome, passing by Melia who was still on the floor, her head resting on my sister's lap, and pushed him with all my strength only to find myself pushing air as he again vanished at my touch, becoming dust. This happened again and again, faster and faster, the magician's laughter genuinely increasing as he enjoyed the game. My frustration built more and more each time, my vision blurring from the tears accumulating in my eyes, until I started to sob, still continuing to run from opposite ends of the cave encountering nothing at all.

Melia reached out and held my arm as I once again ran passed her to try to punch what I knew would only be air resembling the magician. She spoke very softly. "Risho, stop."

"I can't," I said, falling to my knees sobbing, as I saw tears trail down Kaia's cheeks.

Suddenly, Melia's eyes widened and a faint smile crossed her face. "Look over there," she said. It took all her strength to point to a pile of rocks, the same ones I had been climbing before.

I didn't understand why she was pointing at that. My eyes went back to her in silent defeat, but then I heard Kaia's voice.

"Risho look!" Kaia said.

I again turned to the pile of rocks. My senses were not back to normal yet, so I couldn't find space inside my head to reason. Every time I looked around, everything was a complete blur.

"No!" I said, closing my eyes and rocking myself back and forth, comforting myself. I hummed away to a soothing sound that filled my ears while the rocking motion worked its magic to calm me down and eventually bring me back again, preparing me to face what was in front of me. This time, Kaia gave me the space I needed. She let me rock and hum with my eyes closed while she took care of Melia. She would be fine—she was injured by the sword, but would recover. The raindrops still a present from the sky fell lightly on us, making their way down through the open ceiling.

After some time the raindrops ceased and I felt much better. I heard the chatter between my sister and Melia, and I opened my eyes. My eyesight went straight to the pile of rocks that they both had been pointing at before. I slowly walked to it, and then, from afar I could see, hidden behind and covered by some gravel, a speck of hope. Hope in the colors of pinks, purples and blues that shimmered lightly. I sprinted, reaching it as fast as I could, moved some rocks that were covering it out of the way, and there it was, the Seed of Imagination, our flower.

I turned to look at my sister and Melia. They were watching me, smiling. Some petals had fallen, and it was beaten up, but it was still standing.

We carefully pulled it out of the debris, cleaned it up and gave it some water. It seemed grateful for this, and drank it all up, bringing life back to it.

"We did it!" Kaia said. She looked exhausted and covered in dirt, as the three of us sat in the center of the destroyed cave. The night had cleared, the moon shone and the stars seemed to be dancing around in joy.

"Do you realize the help and protection the universe provided to you?" asked Melia.

Our silence gave away our ignorance.

"The rain," she hinted us with a smile. "Remember, the water neutralizes the magician from his powers. There was nothing he could do while the rain kept falling, and with the dragon guarding, he knew he had to get away." Kaia was holding the flower, and we both knew she wouldn't let go of it anytime soon.

I helped Melia to her feet. Both of us gave her a concerned look when she grimaced in pain as she stood. "I will be fine, don't you worry. I will recover in no time," Melia assured us.

All of us went back to where our ship was hidden, the dragon still guarding us all, making sure everything was safe for our departure.

"You're ready to go home. The dragon will take me back to the woods," Melia said, giving the dragon a friendly pat.

Home—that sounded nice.

We got on our ship, looked up at the stars and set sail. We heard the familiar roar as the silhouette of the dragon with Melia on his back flew away, crossing in front of us, waving goodbye.

"Let's go home," Kaia said.

"Yes" was my most sincere and heartfelt answer.

Chapter 8
Discussion Questions

1. Have you ever felt unwanted or not good enough? How does it feel?

2. Next time, try picking the usually-last person to be picked for a team, first. See how it feels to make someone happy. These kids try their best and do the best they can.

3. The greatest magic of all is to BELIEVE. There is a famous quote by Henry Ford:

   "Whether you think you can
   or you think you can't, you're right."

4. Always hold your head up high and be proud of who you are. There is no one else like you.

HEADING HOME,
WITH FIRE IN YOUR HEART

We sailed away, still not completely believing what had just happened. Every now and then, while taking the rudder on our way back home, I turned to look at the flower, making sure I was not dreaming. I glanced at Kaia. She was tired and had fallen asleep under the moonlight. It was just me and my thoughts. I drifted away and got lost in them, enjoying the openness of the vast sea. It felt so refreshing, especially after being inside the cave, where it was so hot and stuffy, and the air was so hard to breathe.

"The world is at our feet," I thought, and smiled as I felt the slightest splash of water from a wave refreshing my face. I began to create those beautiful colored patterns in my head again, filled with colors inspired from the flower. Our flower. Like a kaleidoscope, so many fascinating patterns were forming in my head that I could spend hours changing each creation, one after another. Slowly, I felt a thought lingering in the back of my mind and I knew I was not allowing it to come forward, until at last I gave in and let it swim its way through. I began to understand what the Seed of Imagination actually was, and why was it so valuable to Melia, the magician, the dragon and to everyone that knew about it. Why our mother had given it to us, and had asked us to take care of it, cherish it, and water it every day. They all knew the power of creation.

Then, the images of what had happened at the Drummer's Cave popped back into my head once more. I remembered me holding on to the stone tightly, and I was positive that a protective energy had formed around me and then around my sister. At first, I thought I had only imagined it, but now, with the stillness that surrounded me, I was sure that it was not just me fighting. I had had some sort of unknown power granted from the stone I held in my hand. I knew something bigger had helped me, guided me and had stood by me every moment during the duel with the magician. My heart began to pound, not fully being able to comprehend what had happened. Another wave slapped my face, and abruptly brought me back to where I was standing. The ocean was getting restless, and the movements of the ship were now harsh. This woke my sister, and I could see she was trying to make her way towards me, fighting against the wind. The wind was starting to pick up, and the sails were strongly flapping, almost ripping off and setting themselves free. Kaia was next to me, and the sound of the whistling wind was louder than her words. I couldn't hear what she was saying to me.

"I can't hear you!" I yelled, and squinted, holding on tightly to the rudder that had taken a life of its own from the force of the chopped sea. The clouds had covered the stars completely and the falling rain felt like small sharp daggers hitting my body. The waves grew, and the ship rocked, making that creaking sound underneath my feet. My sister went around the ship, from bow to stern, trying to safely tie everything down, but the movement from the ship was now too strong and it was becoming hard to maintain our balance. At the bow, the mermaid led the way; it appeared as if it had a golden glimmer that guided our way in the dark like the headlights of a car, her face still calm. I wasn't sure that she shone like that before, but even though I wanted to stop and think about that for a moment, the loud thunder pulled me out of my thoughts. Everything was chaos now, everything on the ship started to shift around with the movement, and our flower slid across the main deck from where it had been standing.

"Let's tie it down!" yelled my sister as loud as she could, holding on to whatever she could so that she wouldn't fall. Her hair was all wet now, putting weight on her curls, and her clothes were soaked. I got a rope out and tied it down, holding the flower pot in place. We found the safest place for it, almost at the back of the ship were it would be shielded as best as possible from the strong winds and the rain. Lightning struck without warning, brightly lighting the night sky. Kaia, who was facing me, froze and squinted trying to see past the darkness that had abruptly returned. Rain was pouring down and the angry waves were crashing hard against our ship; still, the mermaid kept her golden gleam and tranquil eyes. Kaia hadn't moved and was standing in the same place looking back, when another lightning bolt struck, and again lit the sky for a brief moment. The sound of thunder made me shake but Kaia stood still, her mouth opening slightly. She had been able to see something behind me.

"What is it?" I asked nervously.

She closed her eyes and took a deep breath, opened them again, and said, "We're being followed..."

I quickly turned but couldn't see in the darkness. A gust of wind crashed against the sails, instantly changing their position as my sister yelled "Duck!" But I wasn't fast enough, and got hit on the head by the boom of the sail, throwing me over the ship's rail. Instinctively, when I felt my body going over, I was able to grab to one of the bars of the rail, and hold on to it tightly. I could feel the ocean under my feet as the waves jumped up and down teasingly from underneath me, cold rain coming down my face, and then I felt something warm trickle down my brow. The change in temperature from the liquid trickling down my face told me what I was afraid it could be. Blood. I started to panic, feeling how it smoothly ran down my face. My vision began to blur, but I knew I couldn't collapse—if I let go, the ocean would swallow me whole.

"Breathe, breathe," I heard my sister say. "You're fine, it's just water," she continued.

I can never tell when people lie, and it's hard for me to read expressions, so I was unsure, but then as it ran further down my face I could smell it, that peculiar metallic smell. I was bleeding.

"Stay calm! I'm getting something to pull you up."

My hands were slipping from the rail. The ship's movements were so fierce and the rain was coming down so strongly, I didn't know if I could hold on much longer. My vision blurred again and I could feel my body grow weaker. I let my face hang back so that the rain could wash my face and clear it from the dripping blood. From the corner of my eye, as I was facing upwards I saw that the flower was loose and swaying from one end to the other. I called out to Kaia to get the flower and tie it down again, but she was right there looking over the rail where my hands were slipping.

"I'm here," she said, out of breath.

"The flower!" I repeated again and again.

"No!" she said with the same determination I saw in Melia's eyes. "You come first, you're my brother!" She was immediately making some knots I didn't know she knew how to do and leaned over the railing to tie me to the rope. The ship sharply tilted with a wave, and Kaia lost the rope she had in her hands, in order to be able to hold on so that she wouldn't fall overboard. She gave out a scream I had never heard before and my whole world stopped when I lost sight of her.

"I'm fine," I heard her yelling on top of the wind. She recovered the rope and tried for the second time to tie it to me as my hands continued to slip.

"Let go," she ordered.

Was she crazy? I wasn't letting go, but my hands were weak and the blood loss was making me dizzy. I looked at the mermaid, still calm under the storm with her golden gleam. A warm soft breeze rushed towards me, whispering, "Trust," as Kaia yelled over the storm. "I've got you! Let go!"

As soon as I let go from the rail, I felt the rope tightening around my body, like a snake constricting its prey. Kaia managed to pull me up using some sort of pulley she put together that moment. You see, as I've said before, she is one of the smartest people I know.

I was safely on deck, but I could see the flower bouncing off from one end to another. We both rushed to it, lay on the floor, and held on to it, anchoring ourselves to whatever we could. We stayed like this during the remainder of the storm, until the harsh movements from the ship went back to a mother's soothing rocking motion, and the breeze whispered lullabies. The night sky cleared again as if nothing had happened.

We were exhausted and continued to hold on to the flower on the floor, that being the only evidence left of the storm, as we drifted off to sleep never letting go, neither from each other nor from the Seed of Imagination.

The warm early morning rays of sun on my face woke me up. As I stood, my whole body ached, I had a splitting headache and a huge bump on my head that hurt really badly, but as soon as I gazed towards the horizon, I forgot about the pain in my body. It was a magnificent sight. The calm, clear ocean mirrored the sky, unable to distinguish top from bottom. The sun was rising, and a few light-pink, cotton-candy clouds scattered across the light-blue sky. A few passing birds chirped, greeting the new day. The ocean was very still, but only a few feet from the bow of the ship, the water began to ripple slightly. The ripples got wider and stronger, and then, from deep in the ocean, a huge whale jumped in joy, surprising me and making me take a step back. It leaped so high that all of its huge body was exposed to the sunlight of a new day. I was able to see eye to eye with the whale as it splashed back into the sea, disappearing again to its own underwater world, leaving me soaking wet.

It felt so good. It felt so so good. I laughed out loud, and the mermaid at the bow gave me a slight grin. I don't know why, but that didn't feel odd at all, so I smiled back at her as I walked back to wake up Kaia and tell her all about what had just happened.

The rest of our way back home was smooth and uneventful. Dolphins played around the ship, a giant manta flanked us for some time and birds kept us company, taking turns escorting us all the way home.

Chapter 9
Discussion Questions

1. It is hard for autistic children to understand when someone is lying, for a couple of reasons:

    a. They have a difficult time reading facial expressions or discerning the intonation in the voice.

    b. Children in the spectrum are so straightforward that they probably wouldn't even think of lying.

2. Have you ever had the need to lie? What made you do it? Try and talk about it, eventually the truth will always be better.

3. There are all kinds of families, and being part of one is the best. It's a place where love never ends, where you are safe and protected.

4. What do you feel when you are at home?

HOME SWEET HOME: HOLDING THE UNIVERSE

The poles from the sails melted like butter on toast, dissolving into the wooden floor of our bedroom, becoming part of it again. As soon as the poles vanished, the silk-like textured sails were left homeless, slowly floating down in a slight parachute bubble shape, nestling themselves back to drape over each bed, shifting to their original form of blankets and covers. Nostalgia hit me and got caught in my chest. I hadn't realized how much I had missed my bed, my bedroom, my home. The air at home greeted me with its familiar scent and welcomed me back with a teddy-bear-like hug of warmth and security.

My sister and I were both sitting on our beds. Kaia was holding the flower without letting it go, as she had been since the stormy night. It suddenly seemed so much smaller and common, but to me, still as beautiful as ever. She stood and walked towards the window sill and carefully placed the Seed of Imagination back where it belonged. We hadn't yet had an opportunity to talk about what had happened when our mom swung the door open, and with a big smile stated, "Oh good, you watered your flower. You know how important that flower is," and gave us a wink.

Kaia and I looked at each other, and couldn't help but laugh.

"By the way," mom continued, "what were you guys playing? It sounded like a battlefield up here."

We couldn't find the words to explain what had just happened.

"Whatever it was," she continued, "I'm glad you were playing. You know what Einstein said—Logic will take you from A to B, but imagination will take you everywhere." Mom grinned even wider, deepening the dimple on her cheek. Just when she was about leave, she remembered, "Oh, don't forget to wash your hands, dinner is almost ready," and left, closing the door behind her.

Kaia started to look frantically at the time, checking her watch and the clock on the wall, everywhere she could see and corroborate what time it was. Once she was convinced that she had it right, she looked at the "fantasy cats" calendar that hung on the wall, double-checking what day it was. I was still sitting on the bed confused. Why hadn't mom been worried about us? Hadn't she'd missed us? Wasn't she worried? We were gone for days....

We were both hungry and confused now, wondering if what had happened had been real or not. It had certainly felt real. I touched my head where the pole hit me, making sure I was not making things up. Yes, there it was, the scab forming, with its uneven texture.

"Risho." Kaia said my name, and looked at me with her golden eyes filled with questions dancing all around in them. "We were gone for days," she affirmed, but her voice held hesitation. I didn't answer back. She was pacing in a zombie like sort of way, her brain not involved with her movements at all. Her mind was in a different place altogether, probably going over every single day that we were out recovering the flower, trying to put things together, figuring out what had just happened, making sure it had been real.

Suddenly a cold breeze snuck its way in from under the door, frosting the floor. A shiver ran down my spine, icing me as well. It felt so cold we could see our breath with each exhale. The petals of the flower began to stiffen in the cold air and frost slowly began to cover the window next to it, crawling its way to the top of the glass, jumping and skipping on several places. Once it reached the top of the window, I realized the missed spaces created some sort of pattern or shape with letters and words that didn't make any sense to me. Something was written, but I couldn't understand it since I can't read very well.

"Kaia! Kaia! What does it say?"

She had stopped pacing, her lips had turned blue from the cold and she was shivering, but her eyes were fixed, looking at the petals of the flower, making sure they didn't snap off like thin ice from the drastic drop in temperature. When she looked up towards the window, her big golden eyes changed color once more.

"I don't know," she answered simply.

"Of course you do! You know how to read" I couldn't hide my impatience.

"Not this," she said, both afraid and intrigued while her teeth chattered in the freezing cold. "It's either some kind of ancient language or a code. She quickly grabbed the sketch pad and a pencil she always kept on her night table, and started copying the inscription on the glass.

My heart started pounding so hard that it felt like a ball bouncing inside my chest. Harder and louder with every passing second. I could not stand the loud noise of my beating heart so I hummed. Still the heartbeat was stronger and louder than my humming, so I tried again, this time paired with the rocking motion. Hmmmmmm, hmmmmmmmm, louder and louder and my hand flew into my pocket to hold on to the fluorite rainbow stone. The gentle warmth that came from it rippled outward like a sound wave, and the same golden-toned light that had formed in the Drummer's Cave filled the room, melting the frost in the window, breaking through the coldness that had surrounded us for a moment. As soon as this golden ripple of warmth hit the petals of our flower, the whole universe appeared right before our eyes.

Time slowed down as it was revealed, while our senses sharpened. The air in our room smelled sweeter and colors were brighter. Outside the window everything moved slower, the flight of a bird took longer, and we could clearly see every time its wings moved upward and downward making its flight possible. It felt calm and powerful. I looked at the flower again, a universe hidden in those small and fragile petals, immense and limitless. Kaia and I walked towards it, being pulled by it like opposing poles of a magnet. The now-familiar music from the trumpets could be heard in the distance, the sails began to rise and take shape, but then, the sound of the doorknob turning startled me, and I let go of the stone. The blankets flopped back on the beds, the golden light disappeared into my pocket, and the universe vanished behind closed petals of the Seed of Imagination, just in time to see our mom's face peek in and say, "Dinner's ready" with a huge smile on her face.

> *Imagination is more important than knowledge. For knowledge is limited, whereas imagination embraces the entire world, stimulating progress, giving birth to evolution.*
>
> — *Albert Einstein (scientist and mathematician in the autism spectrum)*

Chapter 10
discussion questions

1. Why were Risho and Kaia so confused about time?

2. How do you think your life would be different if you couldn't learn to read even if you tried and were constantly being taught to? Some kids in the autism spectrum find reading very challenging.

3. What things do you believe exist, but you can't explain why they do, or others don't believe you?

4. If you could take a fantasy adventure, where would you go and what would you do?

5. Did you enjoy the book? Why?

FAMOUS PEOPLE IN THE SPECTRUM

- Dan Aykroyd, comedic actor
- Hans Christian Andersen, children's author
- Benjamin Banneker, *African American Almanac* author, surveyor, naturalist and farmer
- Susan Boyle, singer
- Tim Burton, movie director
- Lewis Carroll, author of *Alice in Wonderland*
- Henry Cavedish, scientist
- Charles Darwin, naturalist, geologist and biologist
- Emily Dickinson, poet
- Paul Dirac, physicist
- Albert Einstein, scientist and mathematician
- Bobby Fischer, chess grandmaster
- Bill Gates, co-founder of the Microsoft Corporation
- Temple Grandin, animal scientist
- Daryl Hannah, actress and environmental activist
- Thomas Jefferson, early American politician
- Steve Jobs, former CEO of Apple
- James Joyce, Author of *Ulysses*
- Stanley Kubrick, film director
- Barbara McClintock, scientist and cytogeneticist
- Michelangelo, sculptor, painter, architect, poet
- Wolfgang Amadeus Mozart, classical composer
- Sir Isaac Newton, mathematician, astronomer and physicist
- Jerry Seinfeld, comedian
- Satoshi Tajiri, creator of Nintendo's Pokemon
- Nikola Tesla, inventor
- Andy Warhol, artist
- Ludwig Wittgenstein, philosopher
- William Butler Yeats, poet

Analysisprograms.com

Book 2 of "The Seed of Imagination" Coming Out Soon!

Follow me, webpage aggieunda.com,
Facebook Aggie Unda, author and Instagram.

I am forever grateful to the businesses and people in Telluride for helping me raise autism Awareness through this book:

- Bliss & Bang Bang Hair Salon
- Baked in Telluride
- Ah-Haa School of Arts
- Steamies Burger Bar Telluride
- Esperanza's Mexican Restaurant
- Alexander Orthodontics
- Two Skirts Telluride
- Hook Telluride
- Oak Telluride